Dealing with Drugs

Party and Club Drugs

Marguerite Rodger

Crabtree Publishing Company
www.crabtreebooks.com

Developed and produced by: Plan B Book Packagers
www.planbbookpackagers.com

Editorial director: Ellen Rodger

Art director: Rosie Gowsell-Pattison

Editor: Molly Aloian

Proofreader: Kathy Middleton

Cover design: Margaret Amy Salter

Project coordinator: Kathy Middleton

Production coordinator and
prepress technician: Katherine Berti

Print coordinator: Katherine Berti

Photographs:
Front cover: Monkey Business Images/Veer; title page,
p. 6: Alexandru Chiriac/Shutterstock.com; p. 8:
Nagy Melinda/ Shutterstock.com; p. 9: Santiago
Cornejo/ Shutterstock.com; p. 10: Andrew Burns/
Shutterstock.com; p. 12: DW Photos/ Shutterstock.com;
p. 13: Monkey Business Images/ Shutterstock.com;
p. 14: (right) Lucie Lang/Shutterstock.com, (left) James
Robey/Shutterstock.com; p. 15: Radyukov Dima/
Shutterstock.com; p. 16: Monkey Business Images/
Shutterstock.com; p. 17: iQoncept/ Shutterstock.com;
p. 18: Fairy Tale/Shutterstock.com; p. 20: Lobke Peers/
Shutterstock.com; p. 21: Gwoeii/ Shutterstock.com; p.
22: Wave Break Media Ltd/ Shutterstock.com; p. 23:
Warren Goldswain/Shutterstock.com; p. 24: Nikolay
Mikhalchenko/Shutterstock.com; p. 26: Jim Lopes/
Shutterstock.com; p. 27: Tomislav Forgo/
Shutterstock.com; p. 29: Regien Paassen/
Shutterstock.com; p. 30: Coaster420; p. 32: Mast3r/
Shutterstock.com; p. 34: Bogdan Ionescu/
Shutterstock.com; p. 35: Monkey Business Images/
Shutterstock.com; p. 36: Stephen Coburn/
Shutterstock.com; p. 37: Malyugin/Shutterstock.com;
p. 38: Tiplyashin Anatoly/ Shutterstock.com; p. 39:
Karuka/Shutterstock.com; p. 40: James Steidl/
Shutterstock.com; p. 42: EJ White/Shutterstock.com;
p. 44: Creatista/Shutterstock.com; p. 45: Lisa F. Young/
Shutterstock.com.

Reference thanks: chezstella.org for their excellent and

Library and Archives Canada Cataloguing in Publication

Rodger, Marguerite
    Party and club drugs / Marguerite Rodger.

(Dealing with drugs)
Includes index.
Issued also in electronic formats.
ISBN 978-0-7787-5510-4 (bound).--ISBN 978-0-7787-5517-3 (pbk.)

    1. Ecstasy (Drug)--Juvenile literature. 2. Methamphetamine
abuse--Juvenile literature. 3. Drugs of abuse--Juvenile literature.
I. Title. II. Series: Dealing with drugs (St. Catharines, Ont.)

HV5822.M38R63 2011   j362.29'9   C2011-907884-8

Library of Congress Cataloging-in-Publication Data

Rodger, Marguerite.
    Party and club drugs / Marguerite Rodger.
        p. cm. -- (Dealing with drugs)
    Includes index.
    ISBN 978-0-7787-5510-4 (reinforced library binding : alk. paper)
-- ISBN 978-0-7787-5517-3 (pbk. : alk. paper) -- ISBN 978-1-4271-
8825-0 (electronic pdf) -- ISBN 978-1-4271-9728-3 (electronic
html)
    1. Ecstasy (Drug)--Juvenile literature. 2. Methamphetamine
abuse--Juvenile literature. 3. Drugs of abuse--Juvenile literature.
4. Teenagers--Drug use--Juvenile literature. I. Title.

    HV5822.M38R63 2012
    362.29'9--dc23
                                                    2011047335

Crabtree Publishing Company

www.crabtreebooks.com   1-800-387-7650

Printed in the U.S.A./112011/JA20111018

Published in Canada
Crabtree Publishing
616 Welland Ave.
St. Catharines, Ontario
L2M 5V6

Published in the United States
Crabtree Publishing
PMB 59051
350 Fifth Avenue, 59th Floor
New York, New York 10118

Published in the United Kingdom
Crabtree Publishing
Maritime House
Basin Road North, Hove
BN41 1WR

Published in Australia
Crabtree Publishing
3 Charles Street
Coburg North
VIC 3058

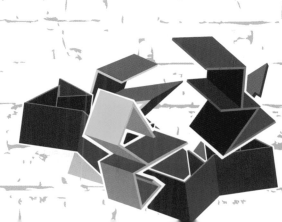

Facts & Stats

Some studies link MDMA, or Ecstasy, use to a user's future likelihood of experiencing psychiatric disorders such as depression, anxiety, and obsessive-compulsive disorder.

After years of decline, Ecstasy use is on the rise again for young people in grades 8 to 10. Researchers think this might be because teens are not aware of the risks associated with it.

A study funded by the U.S. Department of Federal Justice found that in 2007, nearly 200,000 women were victims of drug-facilitated rape. Two of the most commonly used date-rape drugs are the club drugs known as GHB and Rohypnol.

Hallucinogens such as LSD, "magic mushrooms" and PCP have gained popularity among the club and party crowd.

Introduction
Party On

Everybody likes to have a good time laughing, listening to music, and having fun with friends. Would you be tempted if your friends offered you a pill that allowed you to feel incredible happiness for hours at a time? What if that happiness had a cost: frightening nightmares, depression, lost relationships, and **lapses** in time and judgement. Would it be worth it?

Party and club drugs are a group of drugs that are often taken at house parties, concerts, and clubs. Some are available online, while others are supplied by drug dealers. Some club drugs are stimulants, or uppers, which make the person using them feel full of energy, talkative, and outgoing. Other club drugs are depressants, also known as downers, which can cause a person to feel relaxed and without a care in the world. Just like alcohol, downers make a person feel intoxicated, or drunk. Whether used to pump you up or calm you down, club drugs alter your state of mind, which means that when you're high you're not thinking clearly—or making good decisions. This book will help explode the image of club drugs as harmless, and explain how they affect a person in both the short and long terms.

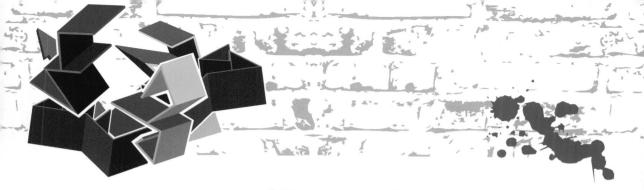

Chapter 1
Good Times?

There are many different kinds of drugs taken at concerts and dances, but they all have something in common. Club drugs are known as psychoactive drugs, which means that they alter **consciousness**, your mood, and the way you perceive, or "view" things.

Psychoactive drugs have been around for a long time. You might think that because of this, they are "no big deal." After all, many rock stars and famous authors experimented with mind-altering drugs without much harm. Is expanding your mind and getting blotto every once in a while really so bad? One of the problems with these drugs is their unpredictability. People taking illegal psychoactive drugs are often taking them in dangerous amounts. They're not made legally, so the **dosage** or the mixture in one pill is always a mystery. These drugs can cause you to lose touch with reality. For example, you may begin to think that everyone around you is your friend, even if you've never met them before. Your danger radar may be impaired. Instead of becoming the confident, relaxed person you hoped the drug would make you be, you're quickly losing control.

Around the Block

Psychoactive drugs are chemical substances that affect the way the brain works. Some types have been used for a long time to treat many different conditions, disorders, and diseases. For example, gamma-hydroxybutyrate, commonly used as a club drug called GHB or Liquid E, has been used to treat narcolepsy, a sleep disorder. Ketamine, also called Special K, is a veterinary anesthetic, meaning that veterinarians use it as a pain-killer for animals. Methamphetamine (often taken in the form of a drug called meth or crystal meth, and chemically similar to MDMA) is derived from amphetamines, which are sometimes prescribed by doctors for disorders such as Attention Deficit Hyperactive Disorder (ADHD). While these medicines were originally developed to help people, they have taken on a new—and much more dangerous—role in the party and nightlife scene.

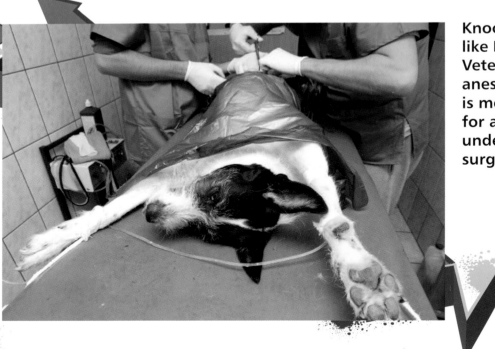

Knocked out like Fido? Veterinary anesthetic is meant for animals undergoing surgery.

I Know a Guy...

Whether a person is taking psychoactive drugs legally by prescription to treat a medical condition or illegally by getting them from a drug dealer or a friend at a party, they are under the influence of very powerful chemicals that can change the way their bodies work. These drugs alter the way we feel because they alter the way our brains work. Doctors prescribe medications in very specific amounts. They also know exactly what is in the pills they prescribe. Dealers, however, are another story.

When these drugs are bought on the street, they can be made with any number of ingredients. The pill that your friend got from a friend of theirs could have come from any number of different suppliers, but it was most likely made by a **clandestine** chemist. This is a term for a person who makes illegal drugs from their home or someone else's using chemicals and toxic household products. They can also be made by drug gangs that are more concerned with how cheap the drug is than how safe it is.

Dealers are concerned with making money, not making friends.

Uppers

Uppers, or stimulants, are popular party and club drugs because they affect your mood and energy levels. One of the most well-known uppers in the club scene is called Ecstasy, also known as E, XTC, and Adam. E stands for a chemical called 3,4-methylenedioxy-methamphetamine, or MDMA for short. MDMA, like most uppers, messes with your brain by releasing serotonin, the chemical in the brain that affects your mood. Instead of feeling happy naturally, you feel that way because of the chemicals.

Ecstasy, or MDMA, is made in illegal labs. The drug comes in pill or capsule form for swallowing, or as powder for snorting. An

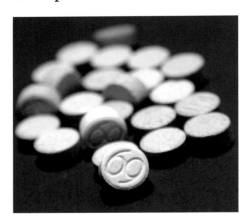

Ecstasy pill sometimes has a picture stamped on it, such as a butterfly or a clover leaf. These designs sometimes identify the maker of the Ecstasy. They also make the drugs looks less threatening.

Flipping Risky

Some party drug users take the dangerous risk of mixing drugs. Candy flipping is a term used to describe taking LSD/acid and Ecstasy/MDMA. Elephant flipping refers to mixing PCP and Ecstasy. Users who kitty flip are mixing ketamine and MDMA.

Downers

Downers, also known as depressants, have a different reputation in the club scene. Gamma-hydroxybutyrate, known as GHB, G, or Easy Lay, is a depressant known for creating a sense of euphoria, or intense happiness. It is also a **sedative**. This means that it can calm and soothe the person who takes the drug. Rohypnol, also called roofies or rope, can have the same effect. Both of these drugs are available in colorless, odorless, and tasteless forms. They are sold as powders, liquids, or tablets. As these drugs are not easy to taste or see, they have become known as the "date rape drugs." They are used to commit sexual assaults because they can easily make a person pass out once they're slipped into a drink. Date rape drugs can even cause amnesia.

Hallucinogens

Hallucinogens are drugs that alter any or all of the five senses. They're often called psychedelics. They also affect thoughts and moods. For these reasons, Ecstasy can be called a hallucinogen, too. Other hallucinogens are ketamine, known as Special K, vitamin K, and K; phencyclidine, usually referred to as PC; and lysergic acid diethylamide, also called LSD or acid. Hallucinogens come in many forms. LSD and PCP are most often taken orally, as capsules or tablets. They can also be found in liquid and powder forms. Ketamine is sold in liquid or powder form. The liquid form of hallucinogens is added to drinks or foods, or injected into a muscle using a needle. The powders are snorted, mixed into drinks, or smoked with tobacco or marijuana.

Chapter 2
Where's the Party?

Many different kinds of drugs are associated with partying and nightclubs. In particular, Ecstasy has for decades been linked to large parties called raves. Raves may no longer be the most important part of party culture, but drugs continue to have a huge influence on young people and their social lives. It is difficult to ignore the impact that drugs have on popular culture. Whether they are mentioned in music or splashed across the front page of a celebrity tabloid, drugs have become commonplace and a part of an enduring "party culture."

Partying with alcohol and drugs has become so common that people have a hard time acknowledging addiction.

Raves and Rave Culture

In the late 1980s, rave culture was catching on all over Europe. Large groups of young people would get together to dance and listen to music all night long. They would meet in clubs, fields, sports arenas, and sometimes even abandoned warehouses. There, DJs would mix electronic **house music** with mainstream pop music. The loud music was often accompanied by laser light shows. Some partygoers would swallow tablets of Ecstasy or other **psychotropic** drugs. People claimed that doing drugs such as Ecstasy made them feel connected with the other partygoers, even if the hundreds of people surrounding them were complete strangers. The rave scene quickly spread to the United States and the rest of the world. Ravers had their own slang, clothing, and drug **paraphernalia**.

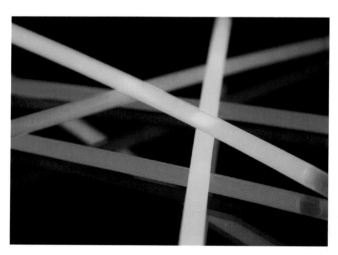

In the past, ravers who did Ecstasy often liked to use baby pacifiers, since E causes users to chew or grind their teeth. Glow sticks and vapor inhalers were other accessories.

Acid House

Acid house parties was the name given to early raves. The name comes from the trance-style music played and the drug often used at the events.

Party Scene

The prevalence of illegal drugs at raves led government and police in the United Kingdom to act. They began to crack down on raves, enforcing laws and passing new ones that made it difficult to plan or attend an illegal rave without being fined or thrown in jail. Although illegal raves still occurred, many moved to clubs that had licenses. The clubs were more easily regulated. Although the term rave is still in use today, they are also called dance or underground parties. Young people continue to go to clubs, parties, concerts, and music festivals where illegal club drugs are available. The name might be different, but the party is the same.

Not all dance parties are drug parties, but the deaths of some young people caused by Ecstasy use at raves gave these parties a reputation as places where drugs were commonplace.

Date Rape Drugs

Not all drugs linked to the rave and party culture are used just for socializing and getting high. Some drugs are bought specifically for the purpose of harming others. Drugs like GHB, also called the "date rape drug," and Rohypnol, better known as "roofies," are drugs that come in liquid or tablet forms and have no taste or smell. At low doses, these drugs can make a person feel uninhibited and lightheaded. They are sometimes used by partygoers to make them feel relaxed and carefree. In higher doses, these drugs can cause unconsciousness and amnesia, or memory loss.

Once drugs like GHB and Rohypnol are slipped into a drink, they are hard to detect. This is why some sexual **predators** use them. They can make someone unconscious or unable to resist an assault. What's more, they remember little—if anything—afterward. Police and drug experts warn people to always keep an eye on their drinks when at parties or nightclubs.

Designer Drugs and Online Pharmacies

Internet sales of legal and illegal drugs are one of the ways that young people get their hands on party drugs. Many drugs, such as prescription medications, can be bought through online pharmacies and shipped to homes in North America. Some online pharmacies are legal websites that require prescriptions before they will sell a drug. Other sites, posing as pharmacies, are in fact online drug dealers, selling illegal or "designer" drugs. Designer drugs are drugs that are made in illegal laboratories. They are often created by slightly changing the chemical makeup of known drugs in order to create a new version, known as an **analogue**. There are no tests done to verify the safety of these drugs and no laws to verify their purity or the dosage being sold.

In March 2011, one teenager died and ten others, ranging in age from 16-21 years, overdosed after taking a designer drug that was ordered online. The young people were attending a house party in Blaine, Minnesota. They were taking a synthetic hallucinogen known as 2C-E. A stimulant, or upper, its effects were reportedly similar to LSD and Ecstasy. One of the partygoers has been charged with third-degree murder for supplying the drug that he purchased online. Under Minnesota law, many drugs related to 2C-E are illegal, but 2C-E is not mentioned specifically. The laws surrounding designer drugs are sometimes unclear—but the dangers aren't.

Chapter 3
You, On Drugs

No matter what type of drug partygoers use, the goal is always the same: to get high. People use party drugs to have fun and feel happy. They may be trying to escape the stress of their everyday lives. Party drugs have specific effects on the mind and body. They change the way your mind processes information, making you see the world differently than it really is. They're also illegal, and since there's nobody to regulate illegal production, no one knows what might be in these pills or powders.

Drugs may be taken by different people for different reasons, but the bottom line is that they're never a great solution to life's problems. Each drug works a bit differently on the mind and body, but one thing is the same—when the high wears off, the fun ends and the problems that you were trying to forget will still be there. More often than not, they'll be accompanied by a massive **hangover**. The aftereffects of some party drugs can last for weeks. Research on the long-term effects of these drugs is ongoing, but much is still unknown. Getting high may cause permanent damage to your brain. That's a pretty good reason to learn the facts.

How Uppers Work

The brain is constantly communicating with the rest of the body. It sends messages to different body parts and gives the body instructions on how to complete everyday tasks. Chemical messengers called neurotransmitters help the body and the brain to communicate. Most "uppers," or stimulants, work on your brain's level of serotonin. Serotonin is a neurotransmitter that exists naturally in the body. Its release creates a feeling of happiness and well-being.

Drugs such as Ecstasy also create a feeling of well-being in users by releasing serotonin in the brain. Ecstasy releases a lot more serotonin than a bowl of spaghetti. It tricks your brain. Once the high wears off, serotonin levels often dip lower than they were before taking the drug, leaving the user feeling sad. Physically, Ecstasy can also cause blurred vision, teeth clenching, increased heart rate and nausea in users. The more dangerous effects include dehydration and increased body temperature. Since Ecstasy is often used in hot and overcrowded nightclubs or parties, overheating is a common danger.

Confusion, anxiety, and paranoia are also side effects of uppers.

How Hallucinogens Work

Hallucinogenic drugs such as LSD also mess with the communication between the brain and the body. Physically, the effects include increased body temperature and blood pressure. Inside the brain, hallucinogens interrupt the communication between serotonin and the nerve cells in the brain. LSD even tricks the brain into thinking it is serotonin. Serotonin affects mood, so people who use hallucinogens experience quick changes from one mood to the next. Since the brain and the body are having difficulty communicating, users also experience strange and confusing sensations. They may think that they are seeing sounds and hearing colors, for example. This can be terrifying and lead to frightening hallucinations, or a a "bad trip." PCP and ketamine alter a different neurotransmitter, called glutamate. Glutamate is involved with the way the body feels pain. Messing with the body's ability to feel pain is risky. You're taking chances with your safety when you can't tell if you are hurt or in danger.

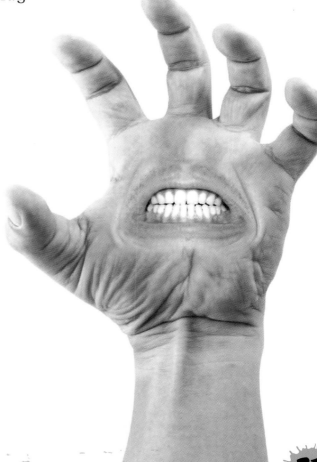

The effects of LSD can last up to 12 hours. That's a long time for a bad trip.

In the Long Term

Some studies have shown that MDMA can lead to long-lasting and possibly permanent brain damage. Evidence shows that once your serotonin levels go down after using Ecstasy/MDMA, they may never return to their previously healthy levels. Some Ecstasy users say that they feel depressed or "hung over" for days after using the drug. This could be because their serotonin levels are so low. Over time, people who use the drug regularly impact their serotonin levels so much that they need to take more of the drug to get the same effect. At first, one pill may be enough for a user, but eventually several pills need to be popped for them to get the same high. Taking more pills, or mixing them with other drugs or alcohol can lead to heart failure, **psychosis**, and overdose.

Hangovers aren't just from drinking alcohol. Ecstasy users get them, too.

Lowdown on Downers

GHB and Rohypnol are known as central nervous system (CNS) depressants. They slow down brain activity and are used to create a drowsy, calming effect on people. They can even slow down breathing and heart rate, which can be deadly, especially when mixed with other drugs such as alcohol or even over-the-counter cold medication. While they are sometimes prescribed to help with sleep disorders and anxiety, people using them as club drugs tend to use them at high doses. They often mix them with uppers or alcohol.

Rohypnol, or roofies, can cause amnesia, or memory loss. Sometimes used to commit assault, the victim is secretly given the drug and will likely have no memory of the attack. People who use GHB experience withdrawal symptoms when they stop taking the drug. Their brain functions have slowed down, and without the drug, the brain attempts to "rebound" to its normal activity level. This is hard on the brain and can cause **seizures** or comas.

Depressants slow your heart rate, and higher dosages can make you pass out.

Messing With Your Head

When drugs are messing with your brain, the risks go beyond what is happening inside your head. The whole point of taking party drugs is to get high, but the feelings of happiness and well-being are the drugs tricking your brain. You may feel that you are safe and happy, even when you're really not. This false sense of safety can lead to a lot of risky behavior. When we are sober, we have the ability to tell the difference between right and wrong. We know when we are in danger and when we are making bad decisions. Getting high can impair your instincts, leading you to make choices that can put you in real danger. Whether it is unprotected sex or driving under the influence, high-risk behaviors lead to consequences that last a lot longer than your high.

Getting high can make you careless—leading to poor decisions such as driving while impaired or driving with someone who is impaired.

Tripping Out

Getting high on hallucinogens is called tripping: because the drugs are said to take users on a sensory trip. Bad trips occur when someone feels trapped, anxious, or terrified while on the drug.

Feeling Good?

The first time someone uses a drug of abuse, he or she experiences unnaturally intense feelings of pleasure. The reward circuitry is activated—with **dopamine** carrying the message. The brain starts changing as a result of the unnatural flood of neurotransmitters. Because they sense more than enough dopamine, neurons may begin to reduce the number of dopamine receptors or simply make less dopamine. The result is less dopamine signaling in the brain, or what scientists call "downregulation." You become less sensitive. Some drugs are also toxic, meaning some neurons also may die.

Nobody Volunteers for Addiction

Although we know what happens to the brain when someone becomes addicted, it can't be predicted how many times a person must use a drug before becoming addicted. A person's genetic makeup, the genes that make each of us who we are, and the environment each play a role. What is known is that a person who uses drugs risks becoming addicted, craving the drug despite its potentially devastating consequences.

You may make the decision to start taking drugs voluntarily, but as time passes and your drug use continues, you become compulsive. Decision-making is taken away from you. This is because the continued use of drugs changes how your brain functions. It impairs your ability to think clearly, to feel okay without drugs, and to control your behaviors. These all contribute to the **compulsive** drug seeking and use that is addiction.

Chapter 4
Party Drug History

Not all drugs that are used at parties and raves were developed for the purpose of getting high. In fact, many party drugs were originally intended to help people deal with illnesses or trauma. Others have been around for centuries and were used in rituals or ceremonies by ancient civilizations. Eventually, these drugs found their way into the hands of people who realized that they could use them to get high. Drug dealers saw the potential of these drugs, and the party drug phenomenon has grown from there. Making these drugs illegal sometimes does very little to slow down their production and use. Over the past century, many designer drugs have been developed, as drug manufacturers and dealers continue to find ways to stay two steps ahead of the law, and make money off the party drug culture.

Back in the Lab

Some drugs have been around for longer than a century. MDMA was originally developed in 1912 by Merck, a German pharmaceutical, or drug manufacturing, company. Merck researches and develops medications and vaccines. Chemists created MDMA but decided that there was no use for it in the world of medicine. It was all but forgotten. In 1976, Dr. Andrew Shulgin, a chemist, was studying psychoactive drugs in a laboratory in his backyard. Shulgin wanted to develop drugs that would, "open up the mind." One of these drugs was MDMA, which Shulgin manufactured and tested on himself. He introduced the drug to a community of **psychotherapists**, believing that the drug could help patients forget their fear and anxiety, and focus on recovery. MDMA was used by some psychotherapists until 1985, when it became illegal in the United States.

New Uses

By 1985, MDMA had become wildly popular in the club scene, particularly in large cities with colleges and universities. People began to call it Ecstasy because of the feelings of happiness and well-being it gave them. The U.S. federal government made Ecstasy illegal in 1985, stating that its abuse posed a serious health threat to Americans. The penalty for **possessing** even a small amount of the drug was up to 15 years in prison or a $125,000 dollar fine. The ban did not slow down the use of the drug. Ecstasy use exploded as raves became popular in the late 1980s in Europe, and eventually in the U.S.A. and the rest of the world.

Peace, Trance, and 'Shrooms

Some hallucinogens, such as magic mushrooms and LSD, have been a part of North American party culture for over 50 years. Magic mushrooms, also known as psilocybin, were brought to the U.S. by botanist R. Gordon Wasson. Wasson was traveling through Mexico, studying mushrooms in 1955, when he witnessed a ritual performed by a Mazatec shaman, or traditional healer. The Mazatec people, from southern Mexico, used the mushrooms to enter a trance-like state. Wasson and his wife brought knowledge of magic mushrooms to a wider audience in a 1957 *Life* magazine article. As magic mushrooms have the potential for abuse and serve no medical purpose, their possession is illegal in the U.S.A.

There are many different species of psilocybin mushrooms.

Robotripping

Chugging over-the-counter cough syrups with dextromethorphan to get high is called robotripping, or dexting. Some young people do it for a cheap buzz, but it also causes nausea, rapid heartbeat, and loss of motor control.

Acid by Accident

LSD was created by accident in 1938. Chemist Albert Hofmann, working for the pharmaceutical company Sandoz Laboratories, was trying to create a new drug for respiratory illnesses. Hofmann experienced the effects of LSD first hand when the drug dripped onto his skin. It was absorbed into his blood stream, and he hallucinated. Much like MDMA, LSD was distributed to therapists with the hope that it could help treat conditions like alcoholism or autism. It was even used by the U.S.A. in an attempt to control the minds of soldiers during World War II.

LSD can cause feelings of fear, paranoia, and panic and no longer has any medical purpose. Taking LSD can also lead to terrifying flashbacks. For these reasons, and because of the lack of studies relating to long-term effects, it was banned in 1968 in the U.S.A. Today, a conviction for selling LSD in the U.S.A. can net 40 years in prison or up to $2 million dollars in fines. Eventually, LSD became associated with artists, musicians, writers, and "**hippies**." Hippies

were a generation of young people in the 1960s who protested issues such as the **Vietnam War**.

Blotters are bits of paper infused with LSD that users suck on.

Drugging the Future

The party drug scene is always changing. Party drugs can make drug dealers very rich. Illegal drug manufacturers are constantly trying to come up with new drugs and new ways to make money. Police and governments are always trying to catch up.

In the 1980s and 1990s, "poppers" came onto the party drug scene. Poppers are chemicals known as alkyl nitrites. They are packaged in small bottles as clear or yellow liquid. Originally, alkyl nitrites were prescribed by doctors to patients with heart problems. Today, many clubgoers inhale the **vapors** to get a sudden rush. The rush is followed by a headache. Other side effects are much more serious and include vision damage and death. Today, it is illegal to sell alkyl nitrites for use as poppers. However, they are still sold in some stores and on the internet, disguised as "air freshener" or "room deodorizer."

"Bath salts" and "plant food" are being used at clubs and parties to get high, too. These are synthetic stimulants or uppers that contain the chemical MDPV (3,4-methylenedioxypyrovalerone) and/or the stimulant mephedrone. These drugs cause feelings of happiness or euphoria, but have also been known to cause panic attacks and loss of sleep. "Bath salts" are inhaled through the nose, smoked, or swallowed. They are sold mainly online but can also be found in some stores. They are often clearly labeled "not for human consumption," in order to be sold legally.

Chapter 5
Dependence and Addiction

Talking about drug dependence and addiction can be controversial. Some people do not believe that club drugs are addictive. Others feel that they pose a serious threat and that they lead to addiction. One thing is certain: addiction begins with experimentation. Unfortunately, experimentation can lead to repeated use. When the body copes with repeated drug use, it develops a tolerance. This means that it will need more and more of the drug in order to get the same high or the same effect.

Genetics seems to play a role in addiction. If there is a history of addiction in your family, you are at greater risk of developing an addiction yourself. Stress, mental health problems, and cultural influences can all have an impact. People who feel they do not fit in, as well as those who have experienced physical and sexual abuse, are at higher risk for addiction, too. While some people may be more at risk than others for developing an addiction, nobody ever chooses to become an addict. Being addicted to a drug also has nothing to do with weakness.

The Need

There are different kinds of addiction. Sometimes, a person can develop a psychological dependence on a drug. This means that they feel or think that they need the drug in order to function normally. When someone is dependent on a drug, they can have trouble sleeping and become irritable, anxious, and depressed.

Other people may develop a physical dependence to a drug, meaning that their bodies have become used to functioning when using the drug. They do not feel comfortable unless they are taking the drug, meaning that they may resort to extreme measures to get it. Physical dependence creates withdrawal symptoms in addicts when they stop taking the drug. They may experience vomiting, sweating, muscle tension, and difficulty breathing (among other symptoms). Physical withdrawal from a drug can be quite dangerous if your body has become dependent on it.

Wanting the Drug

Whether physical or psychological, dependence and addiction create intense drug cravings. This is why some people will seek out the drugs, even if the consequences are dangerous to themselves and others. Seeking and using the drug becomes a compulsive behavior, meaning that the user does it because he or she has the overwhelming feeling that they have to do it, and not because they want to. They may lie, steal, or spend more money than they can afford in order to get drugs. Behaviors like sneaking out to parties and lying to parents and friends can be a result of their need for drugs. This can seriously damage important relationships with

friends and family, but it is difficult for an addict to look beyond their next high.

Addicts may be confrontational and unwilling or unable to listen to reason.

Stacking Up

Tolerance to drugs such as E can build quickly. Chronic users "stack" their drugs. This means they take a double dose (two tablets) at once in order to get the same high they did with one. Stacking is hard on the body and can lead to overdose.

Addiction and Developing Brains

Dependence and addiction in teenagers is an especially dangerous thing. Teenager's bodies and brains are still developing, and using harmful drugs may change the way that the brain develops and functions. Studies have shown that using amphetamines as a teenager can permanently alter the brain cells that are involved in memory and decision making.

Drugs can wreak havoc on the brain's development. They can also change people's lives and not for the better. Young people (11-18 years) who become addicted to drugs often also experience difficulty in school. They are more likely to drop out and are less likely to go on to college. These are consequences that may last a lot longer than the addiction itself.

Want to miss your high school graduation? Stats show that drug users are more likely to drop out of school.

Snot-Nosed and Angry

Addiction in teenagers can also come with a long list of symptoms and side effects that are definitely undesirable. An addict may also experience extreme mood swings and have watery eyes or a runny nose. Their extreme focus on the drug contributes to the breakdown of relationships, and a lack of hygiene or cleanliness is not uncommon.

Mood swings from drug use make relationships difficult.

Chapter 6
Seeking Help

When it comes to drugs, being informed can keep you safe in many different ways. It is important to know the facts, so that you can be prepared to make decisions in any kind of situation. If you are trying to help yourself or someone you know get out of trouble, knowing the signs of drug abuse and addiction is an important step in seeking help. Drug abuse is when a person uses a drug in the wrong way, uses too much, or uses in order to cope with tough situations. Abusing a drug might not mean that you are addicted, but it can lead to addiction.

Your own drug use may be spiraling out of control if you cannot seem to stop, even if it is negatively affecting your life. If drugs are affecting your hobbies, relationships, and mood, you could be addicted, and it may be time to seek help.

Safe to Tell

Whether you are worried about your own addiction or someone else's, talking to someone you trust is the first step in getting the help you need. Disclosing can be a really hard thing to do. Literally, disclosing means to uncover, or expose, your feelings and thoughts. It is important not to keep secrets about drug use. Secrets can put you—or your friend—in unsafe situations. If your family and friends do not know where you are or what you are doing, they may feel unable to help. Letting them know the truth is the first step toward making things better.

Disclosing can be difficult because you might feel worried about unfair judgment, or be afraid of getting yourself or someone else in trouble. It takes a lot of bravery and determination to reach out. The truth is, there are people in your life that will probably feel grateful that you turned to them for help.

Trust Issues

Knowing who to trust is a difficult issue. If you don't feel comfortable approaching someone in person, try writing it down and sharing the letter. It is important to feel safe disclosing your drug habit. If you don't have anyone you trust, try a hotline. A good hotline will have counselors who will listen and not judge.

Helping a Friend

Recognizing that a friend is in trouble with drugs can be a very difficult thing. You might feel frightened for them or worry that trying to help them could ruin your friendship. Remember that nobody wants to be addicted, and if drugs are changing their life for the worse, the best thing you can do is offer to help. If your friend might be addicted to party drugs, knowing the symptoms and how to help them cope are useful tools.
Warning signs

- staying out late
- trouble sleeping and looking tired at school
- hangover symptoms such as sweating, nausea, and anxiety
- lack of appetite and weight loss
- memory loss
- dizziness and confusion

Telling your friend that you are worried is a good start. They may be looking for someone to talk to. Let them know that they are not alone, and suggest that they speak to someone you both trust. It is easy to feel the weight of the responsibility when someone close is harming themselves. It is important to remember that you alone cannot fix the problem. Ultimately the decision to get better is theirs and theirs alone.

Chapter 7
Treatment and Recovery

Identifying a drug problem is a crucial first step on the road to treatment and recovery. It is also important to know what happens next so that you can prepare yourself and commit to the process. Recovery and treatment can look very different from one situation to the next, depending on the type of drug and the kind of addiction (psychological or physical).

Physical Withdrawal

Sometimes, addicts think that they can kick their habit on their own. The truth is, it can be a complicated and even dangerous process, and it is not something that can be taken lightly. The symptoms that accompany dependence on a drug include withdrawal. Withdrawal is very serious. When a person is dependent on drugs to function normally, their body reacts violently when it is deprived of the drug. Symptoms of withdrawal often include nausea and vomiting, shaking, and diarrhea.

Kicking a Habit

Not all drug addictions cause physical withdrawal, but they all cause psychological, or mental, withdrawal. It can be just as difficult to overcome as a physical addiction, if not more. The mind can be much more stubborn than the body. Kicking your addiction can feel like you are losing a best friend, especially if drugs helped

you deal with stress. Think about it: the reason you took drugs in the first place might have been curiosity, but chances are that the reason you kept taking drugs was because of the way they made you feel. Whether they helped you cope with tough issues in your life, or made you feel less self-conscious, you now have to deal with the addiction and the issues hiding behind the addiction.

Old Friends, Old Habits

Sometimes, staying clean means staying clear of old friends and old habits. If your friends are into partying and taking drugs, they won't support your efforts to stay clean. You need a strong support network to live a new life.

Therapy and Counseling

There are many treatment options for young people recovering from drug addiction. One of the best ways to figure out what is best for you is to talk to your family doctor or school counselor about your options. From rehabilitation facilities to twelve-step programs, you will want to choose the treatment that best suits your needs and circumstances.

Talk It Out

Perhaps the most important part of recovery is talking it out. Whether it is going to see a counselor or taking part in group therapy, talking about your addiction and the issues that led to it can help you figure out why you turned to drugs. It can also help you to discover new and healthy ways of dealing with issues like stress and low self-esteem. Many people find that joining a support group is an important part of recovery. Support groups offer a place to share your thoughts with others who are experiencing situations just like yours. Once you have decided to seek treatment, having a plan is the best way to stay on track. It is important to remember that being addicted does not mean that you are weak or flawed.

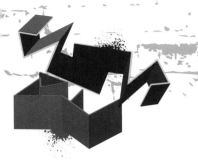

Resources

There is a lot of information out there about party and club drugs. It is easy to stumble upon the wrong kinds of websites when looking for information. Be careful what you surf: many sites give false information and even promote illegal drugs. A recent study showed that 1 in 10 questions that teens post on social networking sites are about drugs. Be sure to consider who you are asking, as well as who might be responding to these types of posts. Check below for some legit sites, books, and hotlines that will not have you second-guessing your sources:

Books

The Science of Addiction: From Neurobiology to Treatment,
by Carlton K. Erickson (New York: W.W. Norton & Company, 2007). This is a detailed but easy-to-understand book on brain science and addiction research.

Websites

NIDA for Teens: The Science Behind Drug Abuse
www.teens.drugabuse.gov
This site gives you facts on drugs, real stories from teens, and free downloads like iron-ons and stickers.

Mouse Party @ Learn.Genetics
www.learn.genetics.utah.edu/content/addiction/drugs/mouse.html
Having trouble understanding the science behind drugs?
This interactive site lets you "feed" drugs like Ecstasy to a

virtual mouse and watch what happens inside its brain. The whole process is narrated, and all you have to do is click the "next" button to see how the drugs work.

Just Think Twice
www.justthinktwice.com
This site is full of info on drugs and their consequences. Check out the Facts & Fiction page to sort out what is true and what is false. Also, do not miss their online version of *Meth* magazine, an amazing interactive resource that shows how the drug can change your life (and not for the better).

Organizations, Hotlines, and Helplines
Talk to Frank
www.talktofrank.com
This site has info on many different types of drugs. One of the most useful parts of this site is the "Worried About a Friend?" tab on the home page. Check it out for some helpful tips on how to help friends and family members.

National Drug and Alcohol Treatment and Referral Hotline
1-800-662-HELP (4357)

Girls and Boys Town National Hotline
1-800-448-3000

National Mental Health Information Center, Substance Abuse and Mental Health Services Administration (SAMHSA)
1-800-789-2647

The National Alcohol and Substance Abuse Information Center
1-800-784-6776

Glossary

analogue Something that is comparable to another, or in drug manufacturing terms, has a similar chemical makeup

anxiety A psychological disorder where a person is excessively nervous, worried, or uneasy

clandestine Something done secretly, especially because it is forbidden or illegal

compulsive Unable to resist the urge to do something or take a drug

consciousness The state of being awake and aware

dopamine A neurotransmitter naturally present in the body and required for normal functions, but also created in large doses by certain drugs

dosage The size or amount and frequency of a medicine or drug

hangover A severe headache or other aftereffects caused by drinking too much alcohol or by taking certain drugs

house music A style of dance music with a fast beat that uses synthesized drum and bass, and is often played at raves

hippies People who formed a subculture that rejected certain ideas and values of the 1960s, and who were associated with hallucinogenic drugs

lapse A temporary failure of memory, or loss of time

paraphernalia The equipment used for using particular drugs

possessing To have ownership of something

predator Someone who preys on another or exploits them for their own uses

psychosis A severe mental disorder where a person loses contact with reality

psychotherapist A professional who treats mental disorder by psychological methods instead of medications

psychotropic Relating to drugs that affect a person's mental state

sedative Something that promotes calm and induces sleep

seizure A sudden fit, or attack of illness

vapors Fumes of a substance

Vietnam War A war between communist North Vietnam and U.S.A.-backed South Vietnam from 1964 to 1975

Index